3/24

OCT 2 0 2017

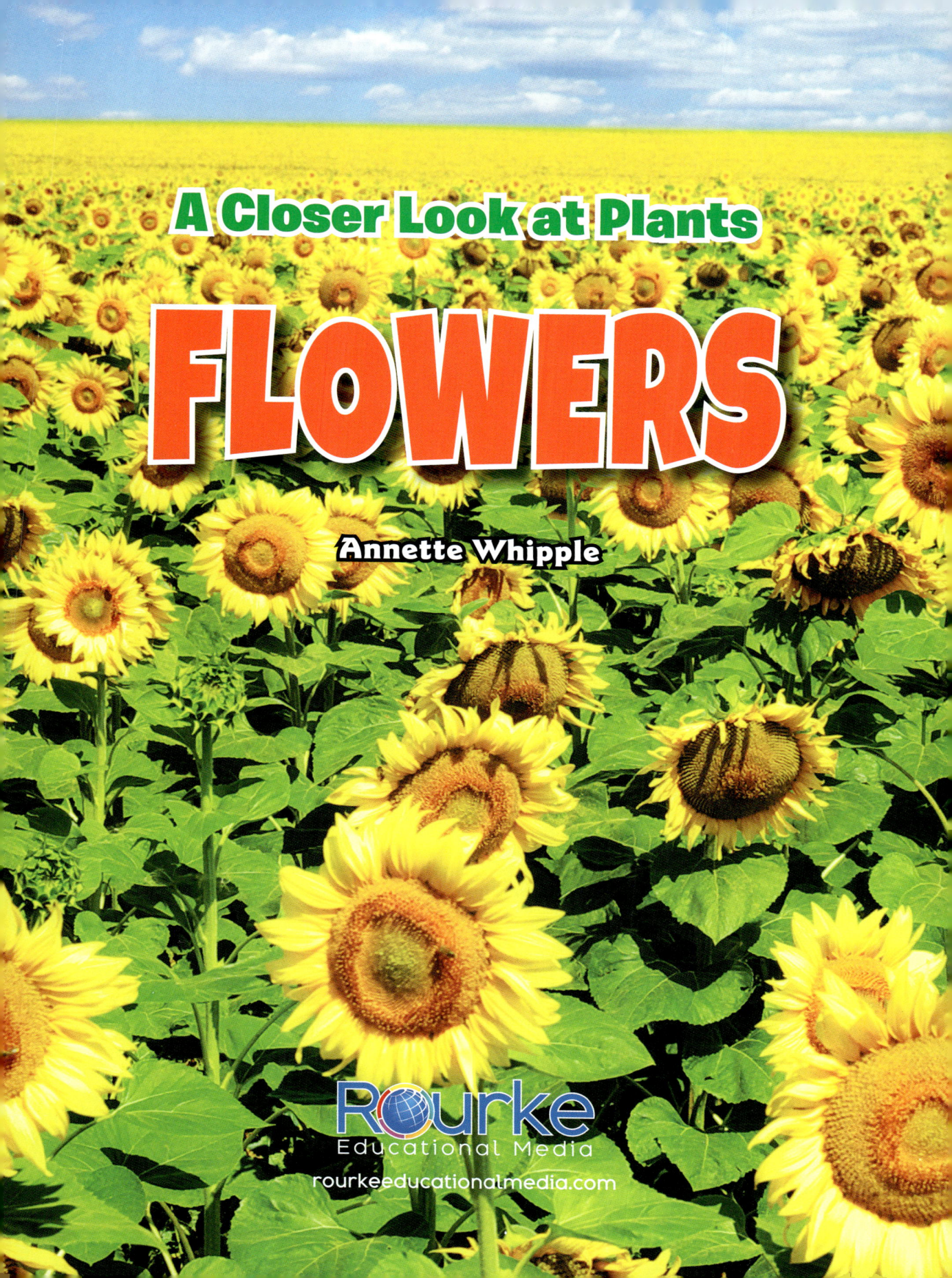

Before & After Reading Activities

Before Reading:

Building Academic Vocabulary and Background Knowledge

Before reading a book, it is important to tap into what your child or students already know about the topic. This will help them develop their vocabulary, increase their reading comprehension, and make connections across the curriculum.

1. Look at the cover of the book. What will this book be about?
2. What do you already know about the topic?
3. Let's study the Table of Contents. What will you learn about in the book's chapters?
4. What would you like to learn about this topic? Do you think you might learn about it from this book? Why or why not?
5. Use a reading journal to write about your knowledge of this topic. Record what you already know about the topic and what you hope to learn about the topic.
6. Read the book.
7. In your reading journal, record what you learned about the topic and your response to the book.
8. After reading the book complete the activities below.

Content Area Vocabulary
Read the list. What do these words mean?

blossom
fertilization
nectar
oxygen
pollen
pollinators
reproduce
scientists

After Reading:

Comprehension and Extension Activity

After reading the book, work on the following questions with your child or students in order to check their level of reading comprehension and content mastery.

1. How do flowers help plants? (Summarize)
2. Why do you think grass flowers use wind pollination? (Infer)
3. Where do seeds grow in the flower? (Asking Questions)
4. What is your favorite food that comes from flowers? (Text to Self Connection)
5. How do pollinators help flowers? (Asking Questions)

Extension Activity

This book discusses the inner parts of flowers. Dissect a lily, tulip, or daffodil to see these parts for yourself. Gently peel away each flower part in a logical order. Remove all the petals, then all the stamen. Next, take away the pistil. Glue or tape all the parts on paper and label them. Expose some pollen by carefully touching the anther. Use a magnifying glass or microscope to examine the pollen.

Table of Contents

Seed Maker	4
Parts of a Flower	6
Pollination and Fertilization	9
From Seed to Seed	12
Fruitful Flowers	16
Blooming Jobs	18
Activity: Seeds' Needs	21
Glossary	22
Index	23
Show What You Know	23
Websites to Visit	23
About the Author	24

Seed Maker

A seed rests in the ground. Inside the seed is a young plant waiting to grow.

Where did the seed come from? A flower!

Flowers are a part of plants. Flowers come in all colors, sizes, shapes, and even scents, but they all have one purpose: to make more plants.

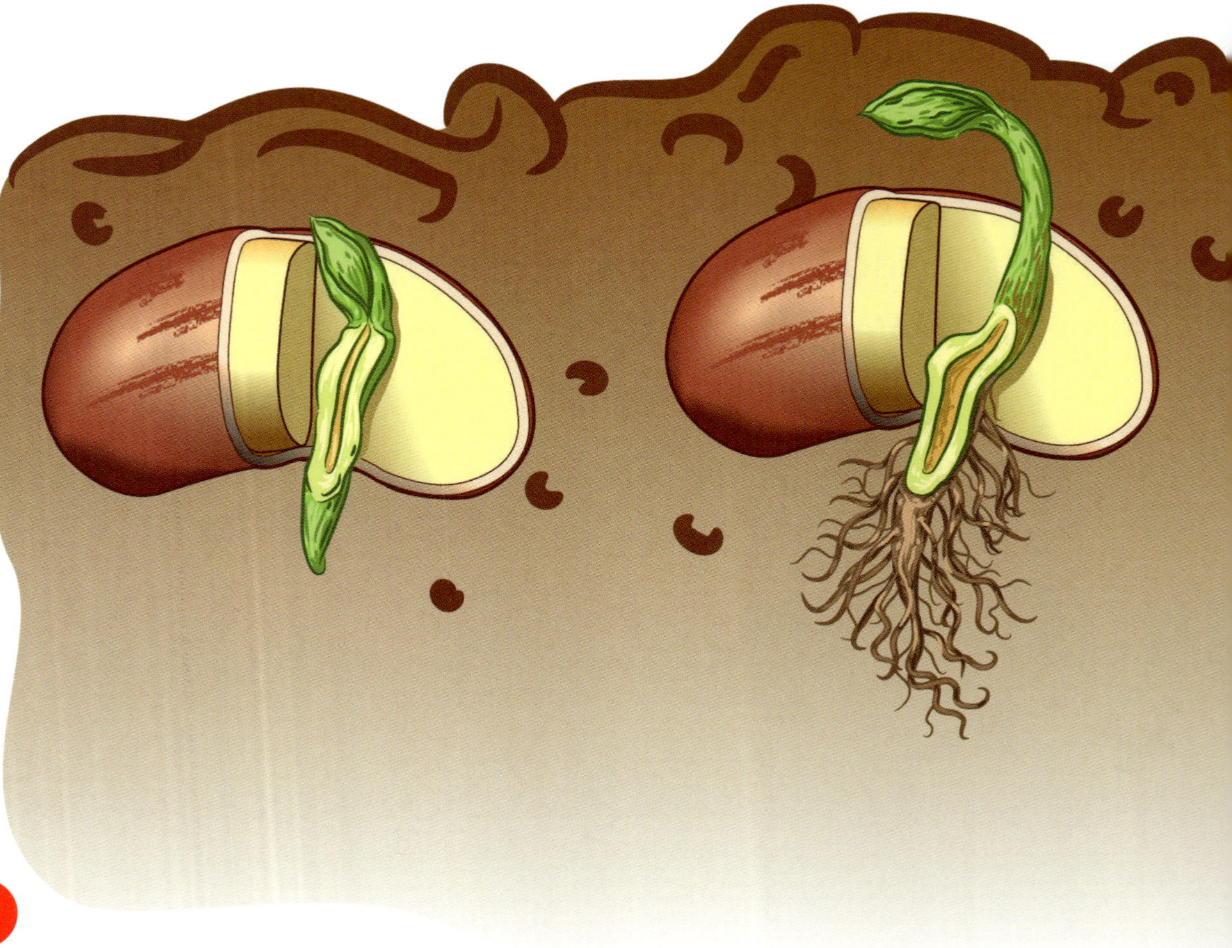

Flowers help plants to **reproduce.** How? They make seeds, and seeds make more plants.

A plant grows from a seed.

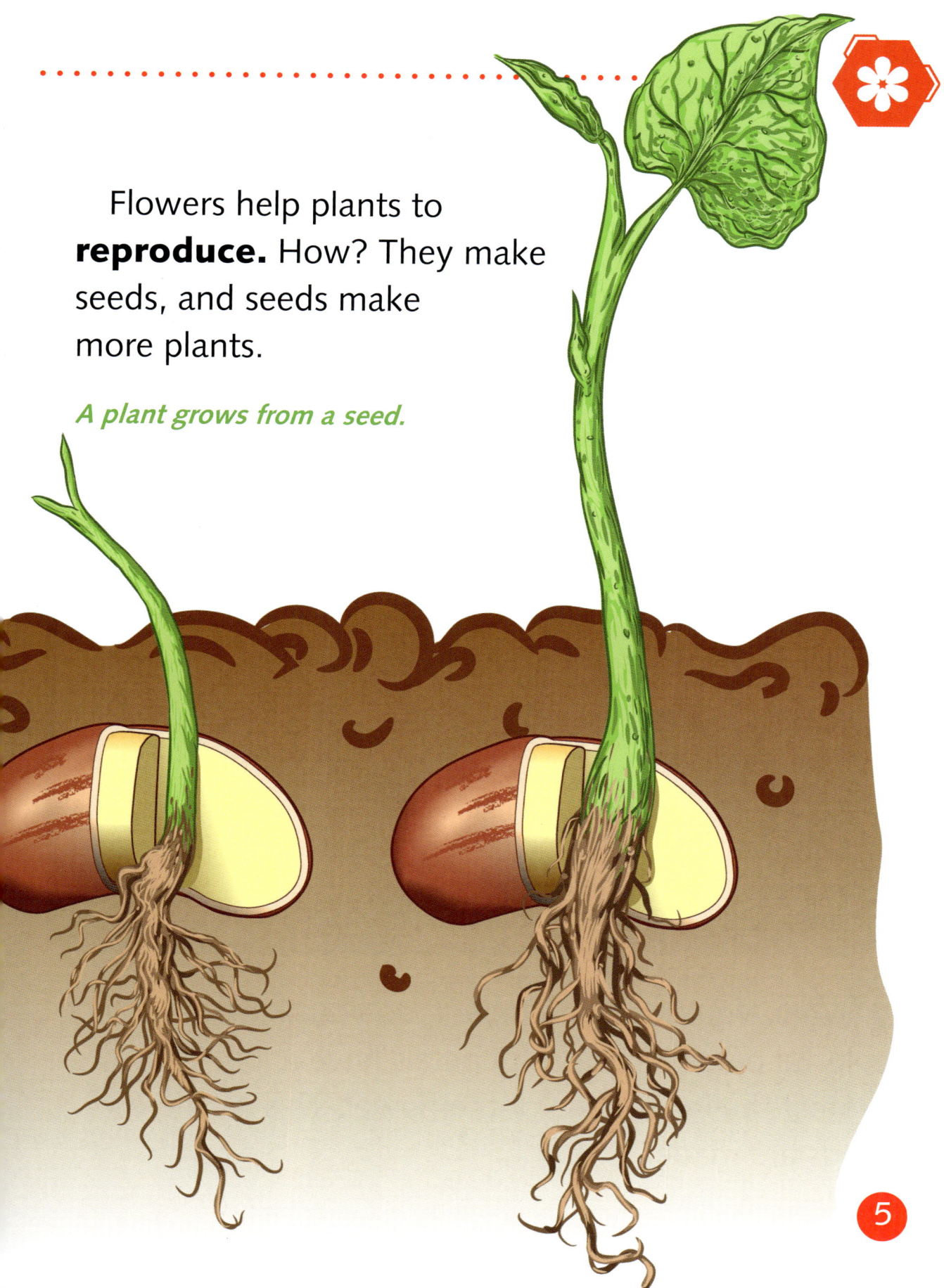

Parts of a Flower

tiger lily

When you think of a flower, do you think of colorful petals? The pretty petals have a job. They protect the inner parts of the flower. This is where seeds are made.

In the middle of the petals is the pistil. Some flowers have many pistils. Others have only one. At the bottom of the pistil is the ovary. Seeds grow here. The top of the pistil is called the stigma. It collects **pollen** from flowers.

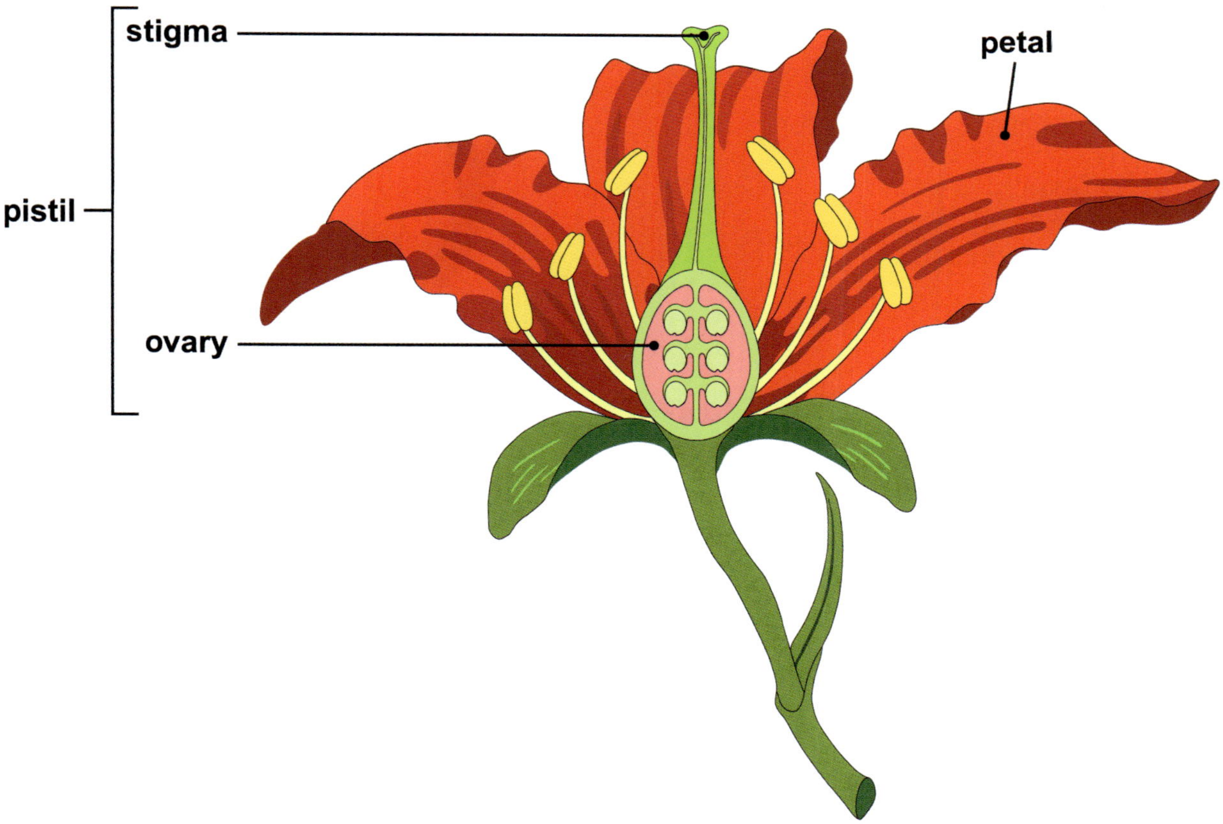

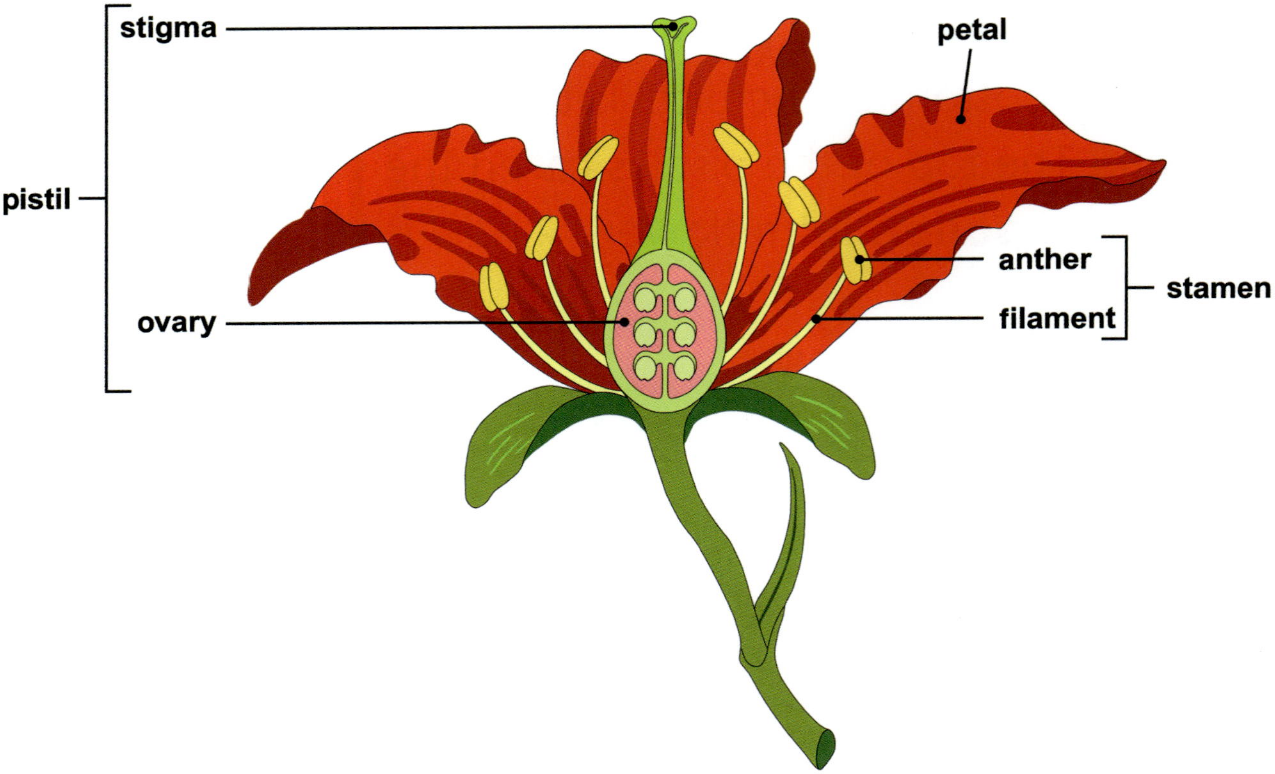
stigma
petal
pistil
anther
stamen
ovary
filament

Another part of the flower is the stamen. Flower stamen grow near the pistil. The top of the stamen is called the anther. Pollen is made in the anther. Pollen grains are like yellow dust. The pistil and stamen are both needed to make seeds.

Pollination and Fertilization

Pollen grains stay on the flower's stamen until they are moved. Moving pollen from flower to flower is called pollination.

Pollen moves in many ways. Sometimes the wind blows pollen. Rain and rivers carry pollen. Bats and lemurs can transfer it to another flower. Insects move the most pollen. Bees, butterflies, beetles, and moths are some helpful **pollinators**.

Busy Bees
One honeybee can visit more than a thousand flowers in a day. Bees are the world's best pollinators!

When the flower's anther opens, pollen is ripe. It must move to the stigma to make seeds. This is called **fertilization**. Then seeds can begin to grow.

Moving pollen between two plants makes strong and healthy plants, but both plants must be from the same species. This is called cross-pollination.

pollen

green-crowned brilliant hummingbird

Working Together

Flowers are designed to attract insects, birds, and animals with their colorful petals or scent. Many flowers need visitors to spread pollen to other flowers. The insects and animals drink the **nectar** deep inside the flower.

From Seed to Seed

Inside seeds are baby plants. They must wait to become plants. Seeds need water, **oxygen**, and warmth to grow. They also need proper lighting to become plants. Some seeds need bright sunlight. Others need darkness.

When it's the right time, the seed's shell cracks. A root pushes down through the soil. The seedling pushes up toward the sunlight. The plant grows! Leaves form on the stem.

seed

Next, a young flower, called a flower bud, grows. Inside a bud, the flower grows bigger. Soon it opens, and the flower blooms. Then an insect lands to drink the nectar.

Some pollen sticks to the insect when it crawls around. It drinks and then moves to another **blossom**. The pollen rubs off inside this flower. It sticks to the flower's stigma. Now the flower is fertilized.

Other Flowers

Some flowers are not colorful. Grass flowers do not have petals. They still make seeds. The wind pollinates grass flowers like wheat, rice, and oats. Even the grass in your backyard begins as seeds.

stigma

The flower's job is almost done. The petals begin to wilt. Now the seeds start to grow in the ovary pod. The pod swells. The petals fall off so the seeds can spread. Soon the seeds become plants! The life cycle continues.

sunflower

seeds

Life Cycle of Plants

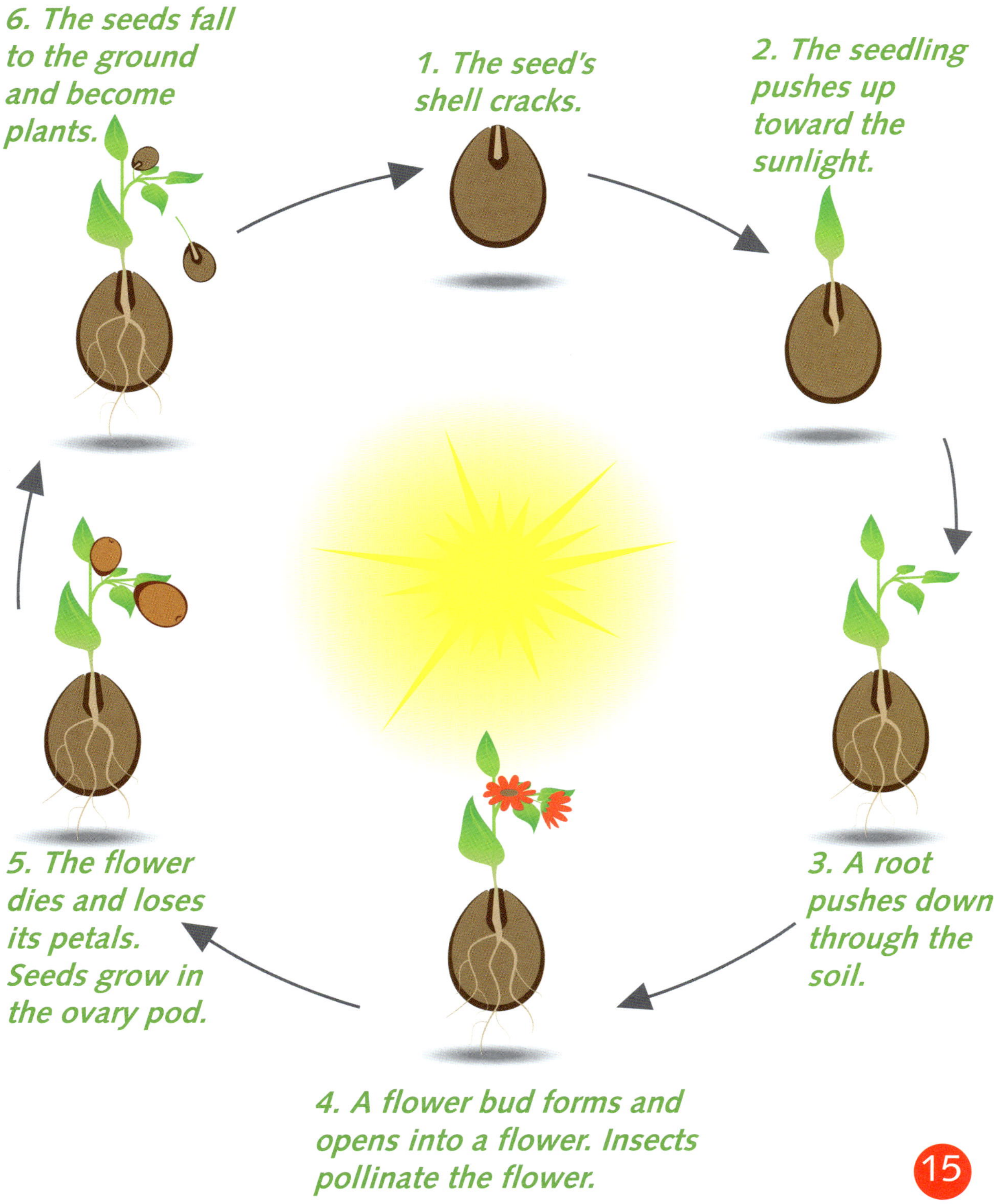

1. The seed's shell cracks.

2. The seedling pushes up toward the sunlight.

3. A root pushes down through the soil.

4. A flower bud forms and opens into a flower. Insects pollinate the flower.

5. The flower dies and loses its petals. Seeds grow in the ovary pod.

6. The seeds fall to the ground and become plants.

Fruitful Flowers

Flowers and plants are more than just pretty. They are useful in surprising ways. We use flowers as decoration and for ceremonies like weddings and funerals. They even produce the oxygen that people and animals breathe.

Plants make food using sunlight, water, and carbon dioxide. This process, called photosynthesis, also makes the oxygen we breathe.

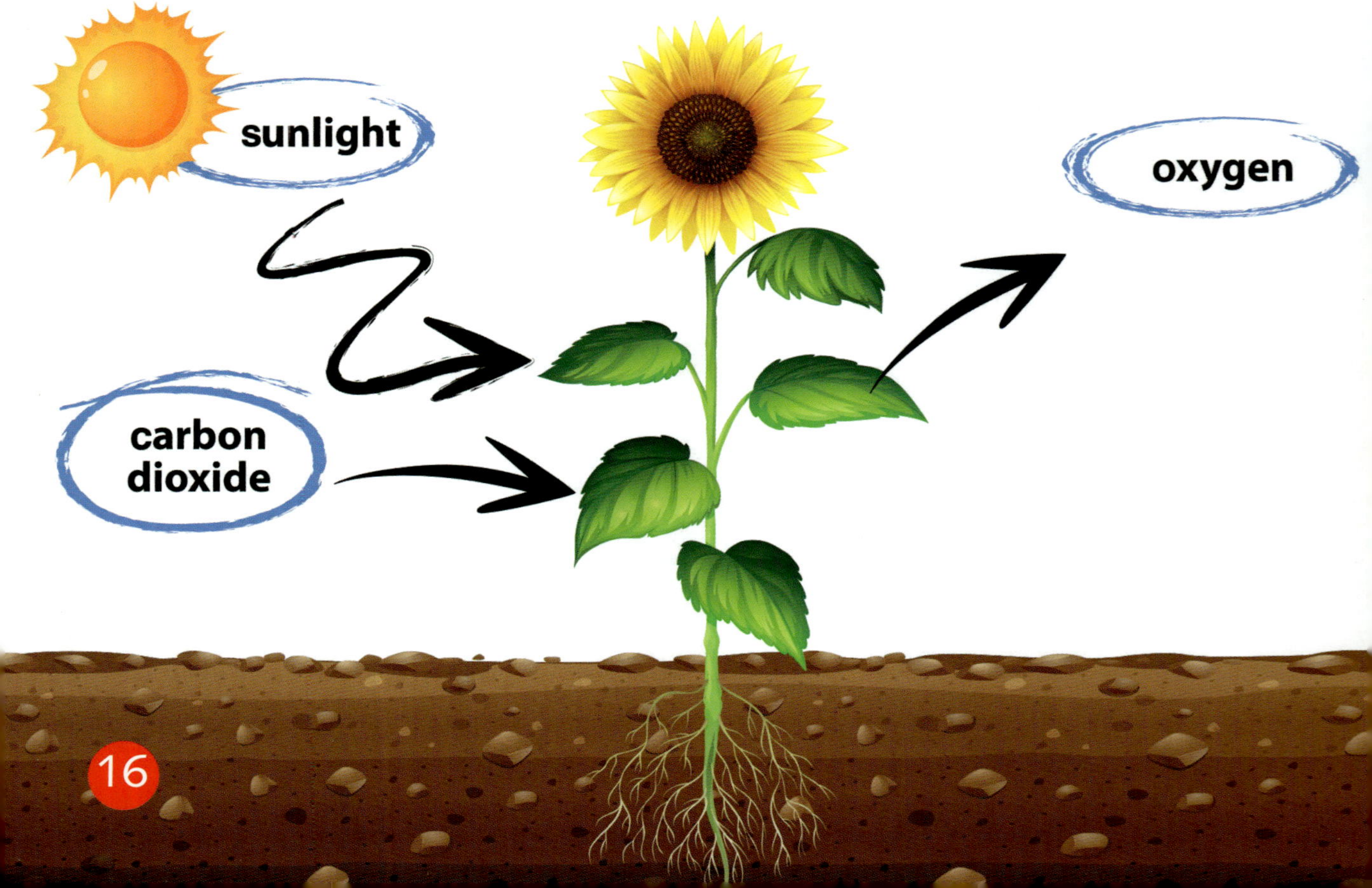

sunlight

oxygen

carbon dioxide

Plants and flowers were the first source for most medicines used today. Cotton, the most used fiber in the world, comes from the cotton plant. Even spices, oils, and herbs come from flowers and seeds. Jasmine, roses, and other flower petals are used to make teas. Fruits, vegetables, nuts, cereals, and grains all come from flowers.

Edible Flowers

Some of the food we eat is the flower itself! Broccoli, cauliflower, and artichokes are flowers. Fragrant cloves are also the flower of a plant.

cloves

cotton plant

Blooming Jobs

strawberry plants

Many jobs are available for those who want to work with plants. Some farmers grow food to eat. Others grow flowers. Some farmers plant trees and harvest fruit. Florists and nurseries sell plants. Landscapers design outdoor spaces with flowers and plants.

Some **scientists** work closely with plants and flowers. Botanists study plant life. Horticulturists study the growth of flowers, fruits, and vegetables. Another type of scientist studies how plants and soil work together. They are called agronomists.

Plant scientists use what they know to solve problems. Some help farmers grow more crops. Others improve medicine, food, and building materials. They help reduce pollution. Some plant scientists even manage outdoor spaces such as forests and parks.

You don't have to wait until you grow up to study flowers. You can plant your own flowers or visit a garden. Peek inside different flowers to learn how they make seeds.

Seeds' Needs

What do seeds need to grow? Let's find out!

What You'll Need:

4 bean seeds   soil   water
4 clear plastic cups   marker

What You'll Do:

1. Using a marker, label each cup with one of these sets of words: *cold/dark/wet, cold/dark/dry, warm/sunny/wet, warm/sunny/dry*.

2. Fill each cup most of the way with soil. Place a seed along each cup's edge so you can see the seed in the soil. Push it down so the seed is just under the top of the soil. Lightly moisten the soil in each cup with water.

3. Place the seed cups labeled as *cold/dark/wet* and *cold/dark/dry* in the refrigerator. Place the seed cups labeled *warm/sunny/wet* and *warm/sunny/dry* on a sunny window sill.

4. Do not water the seeds labeled *cold/dark/dry* or *warm/sunny/dry* again.

5. Check the *cold/dark/wet* and the *warm/sunny/wet* seed cups daily. When the soil is dry, add a little water. Be careful to not over-water.

6. After two weeks, look at the seeds. Have any plants emerged? How is each seed cup different? Why do you think they are different?

What conclusions can you make based on this experiment?

Glossary

blossom (BLAH-suhm): a flower on a fruit tree or other plant

fertilization (fur-tuhl-uh-ZEY-shuhn): the act of beginning reproduction in an animal or a plant by causing a sperm cell to join with an egg cell or pollen to come into contact with the reproductive part of the animal or plant

nectar (NEK-tur): a sweet liquid from the flowers that bees gather and make into honey

oxygen (AHK-si-juhn): a colorless gas found in the air and water

pollen (PAH-luhn): tiny yellow grains produced in the anthers of flowers

pollinators (PAH-luh-nae-turs): an agent that pollinates flowers

reproduce (ree-pruh-DOOS): to produce offspring or individuals of the same kind

scientists (SYE-uhn-tists): people who are trained to work in science

Index

anther 8, 10
ovary 7, 8, 14, 15
petals 6, 7, 11, 13, 14, 15, 17
pistil(s) 7, 8
pollen 7, 8, 9, 10, 11, 13
seed(s) 4, 5, 6, 7, 8, 10, 12, 13, 14, 15, 17, 20
stamen 8, 9
stigma 7, 10, 13

Show What You Know

1. Why are flowers important?
2. Name three ways pollen moves.
3. How are flowers fertilized?
4. What do seeds need to grow?
5. How do people use flowers?

Websites to Visit

http://extension.illinois.edu/gpe/index.cfm
www.biology4kids.com/files/plants_main.html
www.annettewhipple.com/2017/01/pollination-activity.html

About the Author

Annette Whipple learned to love science and nature during her years as an environmental educator and classroom teacher. She lives with her family in southeastern Pennsylvania. Annette enjoys reading a good book and snacking on warm chocolate chip cookies. Learn more about Annette and her presentations at www.AnnetteWhipple.com.

Meet the Author!
www.meetREMauthors.com

© 2018 Rourke Educational Media

All rights reserved. No part of this book may be reproduced or utilized in any form or by any means, electronic or mechanical including photocopying, recording, or by any information storage and retrieval system without permission in writing from the publisher.

www.rourkeeducationalmedia.com

PHOTO CREDITS:Cover: background os sunflowers © photolinc, illustration © udaix, flower icon © ArchMan; title page © meirion matthias; page 4-5 © NoPainNoGain; page 6 © CrispyPork, page 7 and 8 © udaix, page 9 © Christian Musat; pages 10-11 © single bee © pixel, bee on flower © Tsekhmister, page 11 g Ondrej Prosicky; page 13 © Wanya007,; page 14 © Moshbidon, page 15 © Divector; page 16 © BlueRingMedia, page 17 cotton plant © Toko Kawatoko, cloves © Armen Tigranyan; page 18 © Alexlky, page 19 © zhu difeng; page 20 © sirtravelalot. All images from Shutterstock.com except page 12 © Bogdan Wa kowicz | Dreamstime.com,

Edited by: Keli Sipperley

Cover and Interior design by: Nicola Stratford   www.nicolastratford.com

Library of Congress PCN Data

Flowers / Annette Whipple
 (A Closer Look at Plants)
  ISBN 978-1-68342-384-3 (hard cover)
  ISBN 978-1-68342-454-3 (soft cover)
  ISBN 978-1-68342-550-2 (e-Book)
Library of Congress Control Number: 2017931264

Rourke Educational Media
Printed in the United States of America, North Mankato, Minnesota